The Little Kiwi's New Year

Nikki Slade Robinson

Little Kiwi
woke up suddenly.

Something was different.

The moon was shining
deep into her burrow.

"Oh!
It's coming!
I must tell everyone!"

She rushed into the night...

"Wake up, Weka!
Can you feel it coming?"

"No, no, Little Kiwi.
That's just my empty tummy
rumbling.
Go back to sleep!"

"Quick, Weka!
Hurry!"

Little Kiwi ran on.
Weka yawned and hurried after her.

"Get up, Ruru!
Can you feel it coming?"

"No, no, Little Kiwi.
That's just my grandchildren
coming home.
Go back to sleep!"

"Quick, Ruru!
Hurry!"

Little Kiwi ran on.
Ruru, her grandchildren, and Weka
hurried after her.

"No, no, Little Kiwi.
I was just singing in my dreams.
Go back to sleep!"

"Quick, Tūī!
Hurry!"

Little Kiwi ran on.

Tūī, Ruru, her grandchildren,
and Weka
hurried after her.

"No, no, Little Kiwi.
You just touched my silken web.
Go back to sleep!"

"Quick, Katipō!
Hurry!"

Little Kiwi ran on.

Katipō, Tūī, Ruru, her grandchildren,
and Weka
all hurried after her.

AEEEEE!
ROARRR!

Little Kiwi stopped.

Oompf!

Katipō, Tūī, Ruru, her
grandchildren, and Weka
all crashed into Little Kiwi.

"Be careful, Little Kiwi!"

Katipō looked over Little Kiwi's shoulder.
"That's just the wind waiting for us."

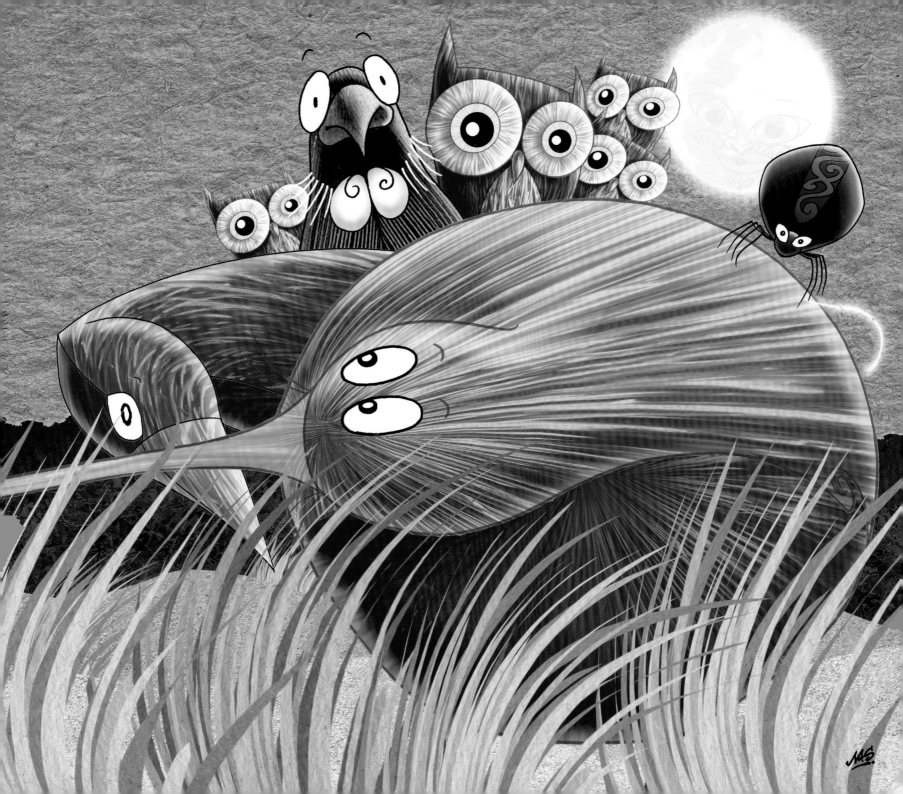

Little Kiwi pushed through the grasses
and stepped onto the beach.
The wind gently ruffled her feathers.

Everyone waited... and waited.

They all gasped.

"The light comes,
and the stars of the Māori New Year!"
whispered Little Kiwi.

"The Māori New Year?" said Weka, "Time for food!"
He pulled a fat grub out of the driftwood.

"The Māori New Year?" said Ruru,
"Time for family!"
She hugged her family tight.

"The Māori New Year?" said Tūī, "Time
for music and dance!"
He sang to the stars.

"The Māori New Year?" said Katipō,
"Time for fun!"
She flung her webbed kite high
to catch the wind.

The Māori New Year

The Māori New Year is a special time in New Zealand around May or June, when a star cluster known as the Pleiades (the Seven Sisters) appears in the northeastern sky.

Traditionally, the Māori New Year celebrated a successful harvest and was a time to prepare for the next growing season. It was also a time to remember loved ones who had passed on. Families came together to share food and songs and to dance. Kites were often flown.

Today, the Māori New Year is still a time to come together and enjoy these traditional activities.

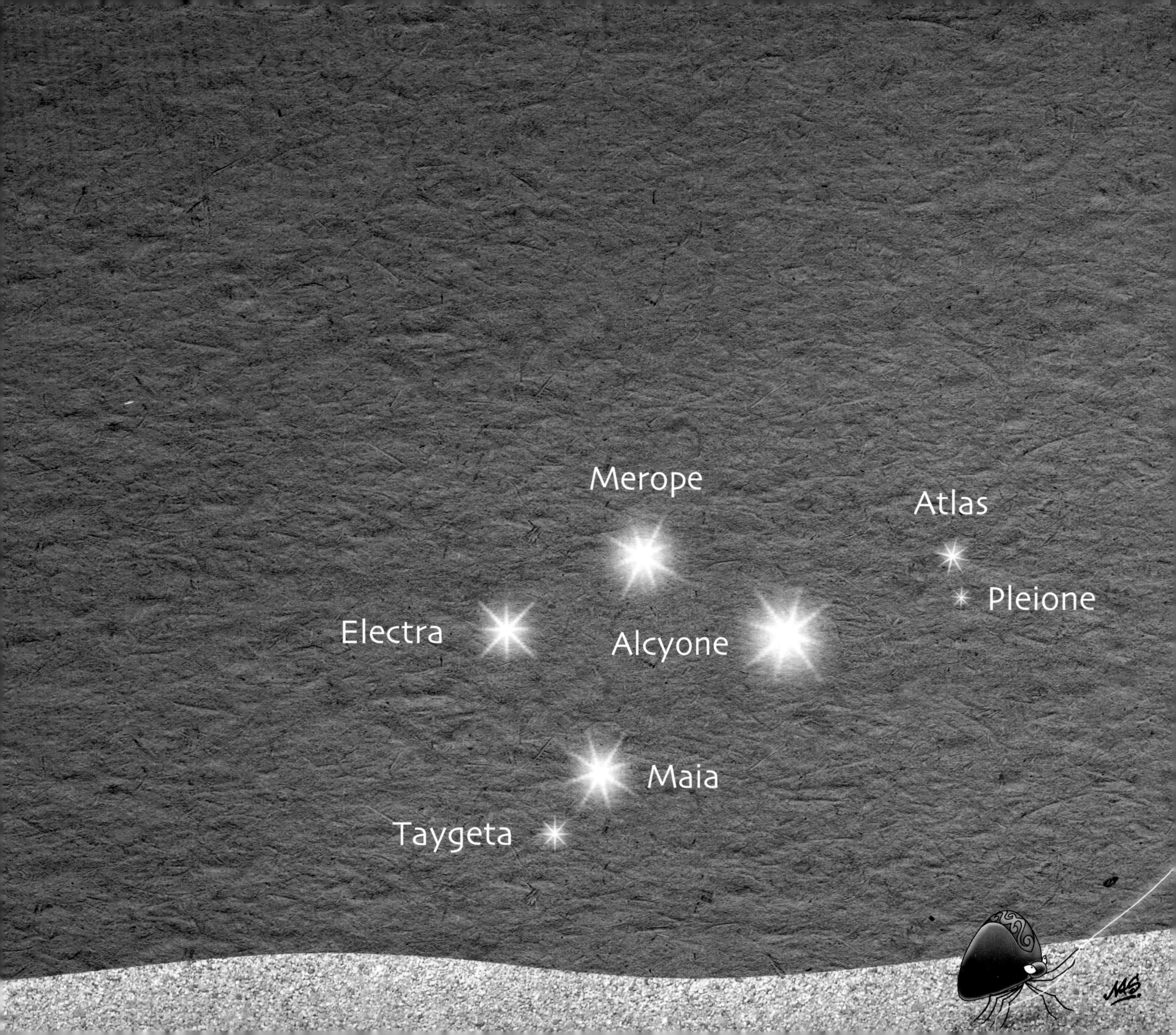
Merope
Atlas
Pleione
Electra
Alcyone
Maia
Taygeta
NAS

Starfish Bay® Children's Books
An imprint of Starfish Bay Publishing
www.starfishbaypublishing.com

THE LITTLE KIWI'S NEW YEAR

This edition © Starfish Bay Publishing 2020
ISBN 978-1-76036-094-8
First Published 2020
© Nikki Slade Robinson, 2020
Published by arrangement with Duck Creek Press, Mangawhai, New Zealand
Printed in China